To: _____

From: _____

"Take care of my sheep."
—John 21:16

Copyright © 2021 by Berenstain Enterprises, Inc. All rights reserved. Published in the United States by
Random House Children's Books, a division of Penguin Random House LLC, New York.
Random House and the colophon are registered trademarks of Penguin Random House LLC.

Visit us on the Web!
rhcbooks.com
BerenstainBears.com

Educators and librarians, for a variety of teaching tools, visit us at RHTeachersLibrarians.com

Library of Congress Control Number: 2020937898
ISBN 978-0-593-30240-8 (trade)
ISBN 978-0-593-30520-1 (e-book)

MANUFACTURED IN CHINA
10 9 8 7 6 5 4 3 2 1

Random House Children's Books supports the First Amendment and celebrates the right to read.

The Berenstain Bears
Gifts of the Spirit
Caring

Mike Berenstain

Based on the characters created by
Stan and Jan Berenstain

Random House 🏠 **New York**

The phone was ringing in the big tree house down a sunny dirt road deep in Bear Country.

Mama picked it up.
"Hello?" she said. "Why, hello, Ned! How's Min doing?"
The family listened eagerly. Cousin Fred's mom, Aunt Min, was expecting a new baby any day. Maybe this was the big news!

"Oh, that's wonderful!" cried Mama. "Congratulations! Give Min our best. We'll be over to visit as soon as she's back from the hospital. Bye now!"

Mama turned to the rest of the family, but before she could speak, they all started to talk.

"Aunt Min had her baby!" and "Wonderful news!" and "Cousin Fred's a big brother now!" and just plain "Yay!" came tumbling out.

"Yes, it's true," said Mama. "A new baby
has been born in our family!"

"Is it a boy or a girl?"
asked Papa.

"A little girl," replied Mama.

"Aww!" said Sister
and Honey.

"What are they naming her?"
asked Brother.
    "Theodora," Mama replied.

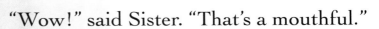

"Wow!" said Sister. "That's a mouthful."

"They'll call her Teddi for short," added Mama.

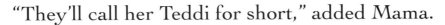

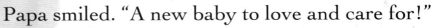

Papa smiled. "A new baby to love and care for!"

A few days later, the family decided to visit Aunt Min and the new baby at their home. So, with food and lots of baby presents, they piled into the car for the short drive to Cousin Fred's house. They couldn't wait to meet Teddi!

When they arrived, they happily greeted Uncle Ned and Cousin Fred. The cubs congratulated Fred on being a big brother.

"You'll have new responsibilities now," said Brother. "You'll have to look out for your little sister — just like I do!"

"Yes!" laughed Sister, hugging him. "Just like my big, strong Brother Bear!"

Honey giggled along with her big sister.

They all went in to see Aunt Min and little Teddi. The baby was fast asleep. Aunt Min was holding and rocking her.

The cubs looked down at their new baby cousin. She was tiny!
They hadn't realized how little a newborn baby would be.

"When will she wake up?" asked Brother.
"Newborn babies sleep most of the time," explained Aunt Min.
"She really only wakes up for feeding."

"When's that?" asked Sister, wanting to see the baby awake and doing something.

"Well, she just ate," said Aunt Min. "So she'll be asleep for a while."

"Oh!" said Sister, disappointed.

"But you can hold her if you want," added Aunt Min
kindly.

"Really?" said Sister. "Can I?"

"Of course!" said Aunt Min. "After all, you're her big cousin. I'll need you, Brother, and Honey to help take care of her."

Sister carefully took the baby in her arms. Teddi slept peacefully as Sister gazed down at her in awe. She was so tiny—but so perfect! She had a perfect little nose, perfect little ears, and perfect little fingers and toes.

"Hello there, cutie!" whispered Sister. "I'm so excited to be your big cousin!"

Then it was Brother's turn to hold Teddi. He also thought she was absolutely adorable! Honey was still a bit too young to hold a baby by herself, but she gently touched Teddi's tiny toes while Aunt Min cradled her. Honey was very pleased that there was finally a family member younger than her.

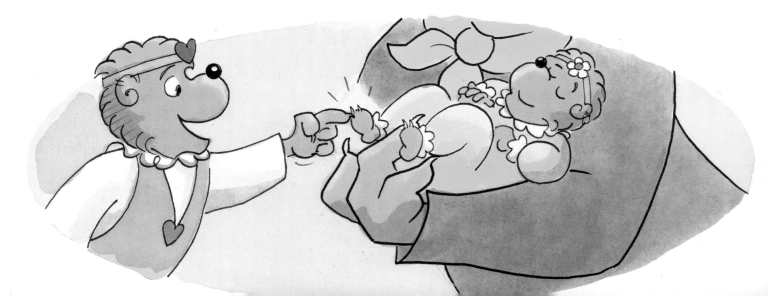

"Baby!" Honey said, pointing to Teddi. Then she announced proudly, pointing to herself, "Honey not a baby."

"No, of course not!" said Papa, smiling. "You're a big cub now."

A few weeks later, the whole family gathered at the
Chapel in the Woods. It was time for little Teddi's baptism.

Preacher Brown sprinkled water on her as a sign that she had become part of another family, a loving, caring family—the family of faith.

Preacher Brown held Teddi out for all to see.
"Let us welcome the newest member of our church
family," he declared. "Little Theodora 'Teddi' Bear!"

Everyone clapped and waved. Teddi moved her tiny fist as if she were waving back. Then she accidentally bopped Preacher Brown right on the nose!

"Ow!" he said, rubbing his nose. "Teddi's certainly making her presence felt!"

Everyone laughed while wiping away happy tears.